# Dear Parents:

Congratulations! Your child is taking the first steps on an exciting journey. The destination? Independent reading!

**STEP INTO READING®** will help your child get there. The program offers five steps to reading success. Each step includes fun stories and colorful art or photographs. In addition to original fiction and books with favorite characters, there are Step into Reading Non-Fiction Readers, Phonics Readers and Boxed Sets, Sticker Readers, and Comic Readers—a complete literacy program with something to interest every child.

## Learning to Read, Step by Step!

### Ready to Read   Preschool–Kindergarten
• big type and easy words • rhyme and rhythm • picture clues
For children who know the alphabet and are eager to begin reading.

### Reading with Help   Preschool–Grade 1
• basic vocabulary • short sentences • simple stories
For children who recognize familiar words and sound out new words with help.

### Reading on Your Own   Grades 1–3
• engaging characters • easy-to-follow plots • popular topics
For children who are ready to read on their own.

### Reading Paragraphs   Grades 2–3
• challenging vocabulary • short paragraphs • exciting stories
For newly independent readers who read simple sentences with confidence.

### Ready for Chapters   Grades 2–4
• chapters • longer paragraphs • full-color art
For children who want to take the plunge into chapter books but still like colorful pictures.

**STEP INTO READING®** is designed to give every child a successful reading experience. The grade levels are only guides; children will progress through the steps at their own speed, developing confidence in their reading.

Remember, a lifetime love of reading starts with a single step!

Visit us on the Web!
StepIntoReading.com
randomhousekids.com

Educators and librarians, for a variety of teaching tools, visit us at RHTeachersLibrarians.com

ISBN 978-0-399-55882-5 (trade) — ISBN 978-0-399-55883-2 (lib. bdg.)

Printed in the United States of America   10 9 8 7 6 5 4 3 2 1

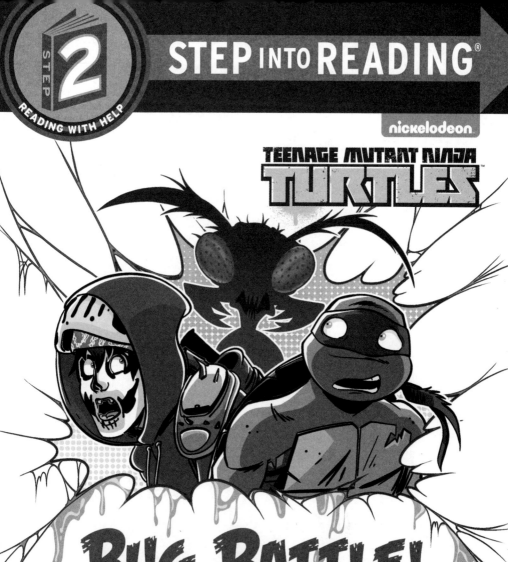
TEENAGE MUTANT NINJA
TURTLES™

# BUG BATTLE!

by C. Ines Mangual
illustrated by Patrick Spaziante

Based on the teleplay "The Insecta Trifecta"
by Kevin Burke and Chris "Doc" Wyatt

Random House 🏠 New York

An alarm rings.
Two big bugs
break into a bank
to steal money!

Raph and Casey

must stop them.

But Raph is
scared of bugs.
<u>Yuck!</u>

Raph screams
and runs away.

He leaves Casey behind.

Casey is caught
by the big bugs!

9

The bugs take Casey
to their hideout.
They stick him to a wall
so he cannot move!

The Turtles
track down the big bugs.
They jump into action!

# Leo uses his swords
# to slice the webs.

But the bad bugs
are big and fast!
They can even fly!

The bugs escape
with April and Leo!
Now the Turtles
must save their brother
<u>and</u> two friends!

The Turtles return home.
Splinter teaches Raph
to face his fears.
Soon he is ready
to fight again!

Donnie works in his lab.
He makes a belt
that will help
the Turtles fly!

The big bugs

better watch out!

Mikey wears
a special costume
for the mission!

The Turtles
find their friends
and the bad bugs.
Flight time!

The Turtles zip past
the big bugs.
Raph stays strong.

He is not afraid.

The brothers work together

to beat the bugs!

The Turtles tie up
the bad bugs.
They take the money
back to the bank.
No more yucky bugs!